It Feels Like Snow

by Nancy Cote

Boyds Mills Press

To Margaret Turcotte, in loving memory of Dudley
—N. C.

Text and illustrations copyright © 2003 by Nancy Cote
Published by Boyds Mills Press
A Highlights Company
815 Church Street
Honesdale, Pennsylvania 18431
Printed in China
The text of this book is set in 13-point Stone Serif.
Visit our Web site at www.boydsmillspress.com

10 9 8 7 6 5 4 3 2 1

Ingram 12-5-03 $/15,95/9,06

Publisher Cataloging-in-Publication Data (U.S)

Cote, Nancy.
    It feels like snow / written and illustrated by Nancy Cote.—1st ed.
[32] p. : col. Ill. ;   cm.
Summary: A woman who can feel the coming of snow continually
warns her skeptical neighbors to be prepared.
ISBN 1-59078-054-X
1. Snow—Fiction. I. Title.
  [E] 21   2003
2002117193

First edition, 2003

3432700215154

ALICE SWEPT THE LAST LEAVES OF FALL into her sleeping garden. She put down her broom and rubbed her shoulders. She looked at the sky. A shiver ran through her bones. And then it happened . . . her big toe began to throb. "Snow," she told her dog, Sweetie. "This means snow."

Now, Alice could always tell it was about to snow when her toe started throbbing . . . so she headed to the hardware store to buy a sturdy snow shovel.

On her way, she met her neighbors Etta and Greta Grillo. "There's snow coming. I can feel it in my toe!" she cautioned them. The sisters looked at one another and raised their eyebrows. "Maybe your shoes are too tight," they said giggling.

"Well, I'll be prepared," snapped Alice, and away she
hobbled, toe-throbbing sure that snow was on the way.

Before the sun set, the first few snowflakes were falling.

That night it snowed ankle-deep. The next morning, after Alice shoveled her walk, she watched Etta and Greta slip and slide all the way to the hardware store in their heavy galoshes.

By the time they bought their snow shovel and returned home, they looked tired. Alice thought their toes must be freezing.

The following week on her way to mail a letter, Alice met up with Mr. Bean walking his dog, Bailey. Suddenly, a shiver ran through her bones, and then it happened . . . the tip of her nose began to tingle.

Now, Alice could always tell it was about to snow when her nose tingled. "Snow's on the way!" she warned Mr. Bean.

"Don't you have anything to do but worry?" he scolded.

"I can feel it in my nose!" she insisted. But Mr. Bean paid no attention.

Alice quickly returned home, chopped some firewood, and brought it inside. Before she finished stacking the wood beside the stove, snow began to fall.

That night it snowed knee-deep.

The next day by a cozy fire, Alice watched Mr. Bean attempt to chop frozen firewood as Bailey searched for the bones he had buried.

Two weeks passed and Alice was relieved to feel no throbbing or tingling. She put on her favorite hat, for she was meeting her friend Mildred for lunch. When she opened the door, a gust of wind blew in. A familiar shiver ran through her bones, and then it happened . . . her elbow started clicking. "Oh my, a big snow!" she cried. "I must call Mildred and cancel our luncheon."

She telephoned her friend. "We can't go. There's a big snow-storm coming!" she squealed. "I can feel it in my bones."

Mildred laughed. "Don't be a silly old woman."

But Alice didn't feel like a silly old woman. By the way her arm was clicking, she knew a storm was close.

So while Mildred was out dining, Alice, who was tired of being laughed at . . . tired of being ignored . . . and not too happy about being called a "silly old woman," put her shovel by the door, chopped plenty of firewood, then made her way to the grocery store.

Before she fell asleep, snow was falling.

That night, the snow fell . . . and fell . . . and fell. By morning it was waist-high. Alice sat by her window prepared to enjoy a relaxing day, but instead she began to worry.

She worried about Etta and Greta, Mr. Bean and Bailey, and, of course, Mildred. They hadn't prepared for the snow.

Alice started a roaring fire in the wood stove,

made a pot of bubbling soup,

and cleared her snowy walk.

"Whatever I have I will share," she decided, and in no
time she was on the phone inviting her neighbors to join her.

The grateful Grillo sisters cleared themselves a path,
then trudged right over.

They brought Alice a pair of soft, fuzzy stockings.
"These will warm those throbbing toes!" they told her.

Carrying Bailey in his arms, Mr. Bean brought Alice a woolly scarf he had knitted himself. "This'll keep that nose of yours well protected," he murmured.

"Forgive us for behaving so badly," begged Mildred as she handed Alice a bottle of bubble bath. "Just the thing for aching bones!" she babbled.

Together they warmed their bones by the wood stove, filled their bellies with good food, and laughed and talked for hours.

Finally, after such a busy day, Alice complained, "My head's beginning to ache."

"Does this mean snow?" everyone cried as a shiver ran through their bones.

Alice laughed. "It means that it's time for everyone to go home!"

"Right again!" they all agreed, and they thanked Alice
and said good-bye.

From that night on, Alice felt bone-tingling happy . . .
for no one ever again thought of her as a silly old woman
with nothing to do but worry.